The Lamb's Bride

Inalegwu Adakole Emmanuel

Ukiyoto Publishing

Acknowledgement

All thanks to almighty God giver of life and wisdom, the source of Grace and inspiration, *My drive in this dive.* By the supply of his grace this piece is a reality.

Gratitude to my family, the Freemans for your constant support, love and care.

To friends in all sphere your sacrifice can not be forgotten.

To all true lover out there my heart goes out to you.

Contents

Introduction	1
The Chase	2
The Price Of Waiting	5
Irresistable	7
Lost	10
Borderlands	12
Found	15
Reminisce	17
Black Light	19
Persuation	21
The Broken Thread	23
Present Past	25
The Black Sun	27
Solace	29
Comfort	31
Ice Bridge	33
Beyound Words	36
The Conclusion	38
About the Author	*40*

Introduction

Over many years experiences have tried to define the entire concept of love, the true nature of genuine romance, as peculiar to some the experiences shared has not favored the masses as the ignition varies in person.

Among the many told stories of love ranging from the impeccable romance of titanic to the unwavering showers of Romeo and Juliet the love outburst has been ultimately visible but there is one that stands out clearly amongst all

A love that finds one even when she wishes not to be found, it chases even when she wishes to be alone, a love that has no record of wrong or interest in the past, a love that sees nothing but the possibility of having a better life.

A love of the selfless expression of true affection.

The lamb's Bride gives a clear view of this undying and unending affection that can ever be found.

In this story the sacrifice of the greatest lover who has ever walked this earth is demonstrated.

The Chase

He sort love in many eyes but found none, on a faithful calm summer day he decided to take a walk in to the country side, away with all his noble escort, he left appearing simple yet noble. He search patiently as he interact with people but the tingle he wish has not yet been felt so his search never ended until suddenly a glimpse of one he had as she walked passed by but his heart panted within his chest as though his been running a marathon, words rushed to come out of his mouth but he could not compose himself, he wondered what could this be, retiring home he pondered, he could not sleep for this stranger's thought was all his head has, eating felt like a waste for appetite was lost, the one desire he has was to see her again.

So, on a different day he went as he kept going other days and for many days he watched her as she passes that same way everyday admiring and never saying a word until he felt it was time then he ran after her like a commoner.

Groom: excuse me please

Bride: greetings mister

Groom.: Greetings mi lady

I indulge you grant me audience for a matter of life I dare to speak

Bride: not intentional to be rude but a place now I have to be

Groom: and there you shall, only but a little time I ask

Bride: Very well then, a heavy heart they say has no joy, speak forth and lighten your burden.

Groom: Thank you for letting me speak, a stranger I am and my form you do not know, closely have I watched and my heart, you it's knows. I fear to speak but love they say conquers all fears therefore here it is;

Like a lonely prince I ride in the west seeking none but only the best and in you I have found one with whom I can rest.

Bride: (laughs) oh mister your name indeed I do not know neither your form have I seen but believe me when I say, I fit not what you seek for being best is far from me.

Groom: my heart has called out to you and you alone it desires, grant these blessings and fill my castle with joy.

Bride: glomouring is your appearance and charming are your words, tenderly you sound and I dare not break your heart but to another mine is given and him alone have I pledged to love.

Groom: broken my heart seems but my hope ain't down here I will be until to me you turn

Bride: I must go now for my lover awaits.

Groom: please, if your heart I cannot have can your hand be close with me for your love truly I seek but your friendship can do for me.

Bride: what say I now oh prince, friends are souls you know and the bond you share what shall this be called since you barely know me?

Groom: the name is a claim but what it is for me is all seek.

Bride: I must go now; my lover will not be pleased to see me here.

The Price Of Waiting

After departing from the noble she arrives her lover's apartment one who has been furious of her delay, keeping him waiting for such a time, he had purposed to discipline her as he calls it for its accustomed to him to hit her at every opportunity he gets. He treats her like a piece of property yet she claims to love him

Lover: it took you long enough to come what is it that held you back?

Bride: forgive me my love, a certain man requests my audience

Lover: and to him you granted?

Bride: it will be rude to walk out on a noble

Lover: and it is not rude to keep me waiting?

Bride: I am sorry my love, only a harmless conversation I waited to have

Lover: and a harmless fool you must think me to be.

Bride: forgive me I do not intend that.

Lover: what then do you intend?

Bride: I …I …

Lover: (stands and began to beat her) I have told you, you belong to me you are mine, I own you and I have bought you, you are indebted to me and you know it's a debt you cannot pay.)

Now if this happens any other time you shall see the evil you wish. You are answerable only to me, should one seek audience tell them to consult with me

Bride: forgive me, it shall not repeat itself again.

Lover: away from me and prepare my meal, my tommy screams and my bones ache.

(The bride went into the kitchen and a dish prepares her for her lover)

Irresistable

As the calm morning breeze blows her hair the glitters and glows of her face became brighter, The Bride on her way off the market, the persisting noble who had followed her many times did as days before hoping to get an audience again, she did all she can to avoid him but a part of her wanted to see him so she stayed.

Groom: Mi lady, mi lady

Bride: (turns seeing him hastily move yet stooped)

Groom: Mi lady wait please

Bride: I do not know what you do to me, I wish to go yet I see me stay.

Groom: ours is not a love of this realm. (seeing the bruise on her face)

Indulge me mi lady what has happened to your face?

Bride: worry not about it for more I shall receive if I do not depart

Groom: a lover you say did this to you, tell me what form of love leaves one with bruises, fainted face and a pail look.

Bride: the kind that grants me sleep and give me food.

Groom: a strand of your hair shall not be touch, your table shall never be empty and your sleep shall be full these and my love I offer to you.

Bride: your words are succulent, enough to make me slip but untrue they seem I wish I could believe.

Groom: you can for the things I say are the things I am, flattery and deceit are far from me for truth is all I am.

Bride: I can not

Groom: but why

Bride: because it cannot be true.

Groom: why say this mi Lady?

Bride: I am not the kind of girl deserving for a prince, perhaps an ignominy you wish to make of me that peasants like me may know their place and never to dare dream beyond.

Groom: forgive me mi lady if it's a thing I said to make you think such but my heart is clean and my emotions are true, my bride I wish you be and until you are I shall not rest.

Bride: very well then trouble your soul until in Deep waters you find yourself.

(She walks away leaving the groom staring at her as she makes her way of his sight, he saw the wind as it caresses the cheeks of his beloved and pulling away the Shaw that hangs on her shoulder, picking it up he ran making his way to her but she was far gone already.)

Lost

The groom came along the path where he meets every time with his beloved but never found her, he lamented, he was in sorrow and in distress yet he comes everyday until news reached him from the borderlands

Groom: oh, like the cracks of glass are the breakings of my heart. Tell me quickly who is it that has beheld my beloved?

Stranger: I watched you daily and your pain I feel, comfort yourself for I know what you seek, the bride you sort is far beyond the sea. Away in the borderlands there she may be.

Groom: your news warms my heart as fires to the flesh, on my way I must be as her memory is still fresh.

Stranger: forgive me oh noble but this i must ask, what kind of a prince seeks a lady like that, cast out she runs from one man to the next, like a bird under rain seeking shelters in nest?

Groom: your feelings I care but your concern is lost, the bride I seek is not one robust, as much as I will, you will not understand explaining to you is only a waste of time.

Stranger: I beseech you tell me please

Groom: the love that drives me is beyond the eyes, it's like the flow of a river, it does not care what's before it, who wish it well or not, it brings its waters to still bless both found and lost.

You will not understand oh stranger but when the tingles in your heart calls only one name and the dream you have has only one face then indeed love has happened to you.

My thanks are with you but on my way, I must be.

(he walks away journey in to the borderlands)

Borderlands

The groom journeyed across seas and coastlands finally arriving at the borderlands with nothing but the forgotten Shaw that fell off his beloved, he has no Idea where to go or who to talk to, lost and confuse he looked carefully around hoping to find one who could help him, then suddenly comes this young mugger but unknown to him

Mugger: forgive me mister, I cannot help but noticed you are lost

Groom: I am indeed lost, the journey I made has no map and only my heart have I followed

Mugger: I see, a woman you seek

Groom: true a woman I seek.

Mugger: tell me about her, perhaps I might be of help finding her

Groom: oh, forgive me mister I do not wish to burden you with the agony of my heart, I trust other thing you have to do

Mugger: a world as vast as this, helping others is sure my *other things*. Go on tell me

Groom: very well then, I seek a woman whose eyes are blue as the sea and whose lips are red as the morning rose her hair is as dark as the raven's black, her beauty is unmatchable.

Mugger: hmmmm a woman so unique you've described, I bet I have seen her and a young man few days ago.

Groom: I beseech you please lead me to her.

Mugger: follow me.

(the mugger took the noble prince across a lonely path were his mugging colleagues where, the muggers eventually surrounded him and asked him to relinquish all he has. Given them all his money and expensive jewelry they insisted on taking the Shaw but his refusal led to a trashing that left him with many bruises yet he refused to relinquish the Shaw, while he was been trashed a good fellow came around.)

Fellow: hey, hey stop that

(the muggers ran away living the noble half dead the fellow picked the noble took him to his home and nursed him, on his recovery the fellow asked)

Fellow: what were you doing along that path are you not aware where you were?

Groom: many thanks to you for saving me, but I do not know a soul or a place here.

Fellow: what then brought you to this region?

Groom: I have followed my heart

Fellow: let me guess, your heart followed a woman?

Groom: in deed

Fellow: speak of her perhaps I may know her

Groom: this Shaw is all I have of her

(the fellow took the Shaw and examined it and found an emblem known to him)

Fellow: I think I might know to whom this belong, there is a family long ago known for their wealth and ego but tragedy struck and they all died leaving their last-born son to watch over all they have, come I can show there to you.

Groom: thank you so much I do not know how to thank you.

(they both head out as he made his way to the lover's mansion for the emblem was of the lover's family.)

Found

By the help of the fellow he located his beloved who was been beaten in the house of her lover, her beauty gradually fades as her confidence too was lost, her self-esteem was completely gone and she felt she's worth nothing more than, all she had are regrets for following her lover, her only prayer is for a knight to ride and steal her away. It was at this time the groom breaks down her lover's door

Groom: enough, her choice of you was out of love but nothing you know about that word.

Lover: and who is this?

Groom: I am he of whom she's been waiting (picking her up) I am her knight in shining armor and I have come to take her away.

Lover: (laughs) and you think away she wants to go?

Groom: mi lady, make your choice and be free.

(She looks at her lover and falls straight on the chest of the groom)

Lover: you know you cannot go, a debt you owe and that you must pay else your life be gone from you.

Groom: name your price and her debt be paid

Lover: oh, how ignorant you are yet a hero you call yourself, her debt is not of money for greater she owes than money can pay

Groom; whatever be it, I vow to pay, mi lady come with me

(Away the groom and her bride went)

Reminisce

The bride on reaching home to the county side reunited with her friend, they both swam in an ocean made of tears for their joy was unstoppable, the bride recounted her salvation experience as her friend demanded.

Friend: the light of your face has return, bold is your smile and your confidence is seen, engage me, what is this that Has happened

Bride: far away in the borderlands where my hope of life was lost, a slave I became darkened by the dark summer sun, songs of sorrow were bread to me, the life of solo was all I live, I could feel the blows of the air and the mockeries of the wind for the choice I made of the one I called beloved.

Tears were my meal as torn as I was, ruptured by men from dusk to dusk, beaten battered and broken left to die my beloved has bid me when suddenly the sound changed, a new song played and like in the tales a knight came calling my name, he kicks down the Wall door, lighted my face took me by his hand and gave me a new name.

Friend: Happy indeed I am for you, true happiness has thou found for indeed an illusion you've lived but here true love is seen.

Bride: indeed, rejoice with me for my joy knows no bounds

Friend: of course this shall be to us a new song and on the day you wed my voice shall give it melody

Bride: my Knight has requested I make myself ready away he wishes to take me, if you will excuse I must be gone.

Friend: very well then see you in glamour.

(she departed excitedly as she runs off her Groom)

Black Light

After sharing a heartfelt romance duty has called this noble and away he is about to go leaving his bride a lone not knowing how long he shall be gone

Groom: blessed is the day, the delight of my heart has not only been seen but beheld.

Bride: blessed I am that your tenderness has found me.

Groom: eyes like the rays of the sun sparkles like the glow in the moon what a creation my father has made.

Bride: yet despised, rejected and abandoned by men, left to roam lonely and alone in this vast exile of pilgrimage.

Groom: say no more my love, hold your peace for this vow I make, yours I shall be even till the end.

Bride: how delighted I am, how gladdened is my heart, like a dream my night mares are over, marry me now my love, take me away and your bride I shall be.

Groom: oh how slow is the speed of light when it compares my desires, making you my bride is all I live to do, but first I must go, a journey I must make.

Bride: Ahh my sorrow shall begin, how sad shall I become

Groom: far be it from me to make you sorrowful, I shall but a little while be gone, and in no time, I shall be here. Take this my love, hold this as my token, lose it not when I return I shall bring a reward.

Bride: hurry then my love lest my heart stop, hurry now for here I shall be.

(embraces passionately)

Persuation

It's been so long since the noble left and he has not returned leaving his bride helpless in the hands of another admirer

Accuser: it's been three years, promises made are now vows broken, where is he of whom you speak, where is your delight in whom is love?

Bride: add me no sorrow for now my heart is broken.

Accuser: come away with me, I shall make you mine, pull off that dress and gain your freedom how stuck are you not able to roam.

Light: let her be for her choice is hers and hers to make.

Accuser: listen to me, your life is yours and none to decide, break free and with me do reside, for all you want I shall provide

Light: alas blasphemer she is betrothed to another, be gone for she isn't yours

Accuser: how can he see a diamond in this rough, not a single beauty not even one to behold

Light: it Is called love!!

Bride: scattered like seed is the way of my life, unworthy I am yet he makes me his bride, when casted by all he pulls me aside oh how now shall I live and bid him goodbye

Accuser: he is gone and no more coming, set yourself free, take the life I offer and be like other maidens.

Bride: my beloved lies not for his heart is with me, it may be long but I know he will come, a token is given and a reward is promised. "hold fast to what you have for soon I shall come and I shall come with my reward" and this were his words.

Light: do be gone oh accuser for indeed he'll come as he has spoken.

The Broken Thread

The impatience of the bride grew like the rapid growth of a tumor, a change of life she made, as light checked on her she was someone different and she never thought she would see her groom again.

Light: beloved what has become of you, how has your light turn this dark and your shine is now shame

Bride: condemn me not for my guilt is as my innocence. I wait in peril I wait in sorrow yet a light so promised is a light now vanished

Light: oh beloved how say you this, you know better than all his words are his he says will come and come he shall.

Bride: a token was given and a promise was made, a promise he made and a vow I kept yet his face is veiled but my heart is stayed. Tell me o light what would you have me do?

Light: believe me when I say as bright as I am my mouth is dumped but all that I know is that he will come.

(groom coming wearing a shining armor as a knight who just returned from victory)

Groom: my days turn night as noon turns dark for the eyes of my beloved I have not seen

Bride: woo be unto me for your trust I have lost and your love I am unworthy

Groom: a promise I made.

Bride: and a promise you kept but here my heart and your words I lost. Cast me away and be gone from me for I am undeserving of the love you've shown.

Groom: what kind of a lover will I be if I understand not what you've been through, perhaps the blame I share for the journey was long and the fight was dare.

Bride: I amounted to nothing until you found me, the meaning of my life is in the love you've shown, tell me, what now shall I do and how shall I live?

Groom: my heart sings and one name alone it calls, fighting the enemy I won, pulling through the storm I came and all to see your face. Brace yourself my love to my father I go, make yourself ready and for a wedding banquet I shall return.

Bride: oh brightness of light, the stillness of a troubled soul how calm your voice have made me and how assuring I feel. I shall make myself again and one more time a bride I shall be.

Groom: fear not my love our story transcends this realm and our love shall be read by many, giving I shall give all but on my horse shall we ride till our story is found in lore.

Present Past

The price to be paid has summon the sitting of the judge the death of the bride is about to be decided for her debt is due to be payed.

Accuser: brace yourself oh light for against you I have brought a case.

Light: who are you to summon me, cast out and abandoned of the father for the sins of your heart has denied you access.

Accuser: long before your birth the constellations were formed and laws of righteousness were established and on this foundation this hearing is called.

Judge: silence, the assembly is for the debate of two rivals, tell us what you have or be gone for weightier matters await.

Accuser: the son of the stars has brought it shame for the choice he has made adds no gain.

Light: who are you to question his choice, the love he sort was the love he found

Accuser: every life has a tag, a slave she is and a slave she's been, freedom is far until she's redeemed

Light: very well then redemption it is.

Judge: The all father made from time that all lives must fall in line, it's no tale that one must pay all that is owed to the last dime.

Light: your honor, my prince I know, a noble he is, he will not rest until her price is paid.

Judge: oh, light so little you know, the price to pay is her life itself for things she's done and her ears deaf.

Accuser: oh, righteous judge, I trust your judgement be true and her life be gone.

(In the middle of the Argument the groom walked in)

Groom: your honor, from the all father I bring this case, (he opens a scroll and read from it) "in a case of love the life of one can be given for another for the price to pay if he so desires".

Judge: do you understand the magnitude of your petition? Her life be speared and yours be lost. Stripped of all glory and honor be gone?

Groom: I have known to live only for her, in life and in death her living is mine, how shall I breath without her there why shall I live when she's not here, take my life and let her live for in her my life is seen.

Judge: very well then by the decree of the all father, a sacrifice of love shall be echoed in time

 And Even beyond shall the two lived, both in life and in death.

This hearing is over.

The Black Sun

The groomed returned from the all father with a broken heart from the rule in the court room, meeting his bride he found solace in her yet knew he could only be with her for a little time, they both walked by the sea shore as they held hands in silence allowing only their hearts to communicate, the sadness on his face shone on his bride and she knew something was wrong

Bride: my lord we've be walking for quite some time but only your silence has been my companion, tell me what borders you?

Groom: how slowly a flower bloomed and how quickly it fades.

Bride: your words leaves in me a depth of sorrow yet what it means I do not know

Groom: listen to me, loving you has been for me the best experience, in this life and even in the next I shall choose to be with you.

Bride: the only gift I got from my parents before they abandoned me were words like this, tell me do you wish to leave me too?

Groom: far be it from me to, your thought is my daily breath, seeing you is food for my soul and leaving you is death to me

Bride: then why these words?

Groom: I swear it to you today, my love for you shall never end, until the moon turns red and the sun turns blood I will love you till the oceans are dust.

Bride: as thunder and lightning journeys on same wings so shall my life be by yours.

Groom: as the flowers take root downwards

Bride: and buds it beauty upwards

Both: so shall our love bloom even in all gloom

Groom: a promise I leave with you, my love from you shall never depart.

Bride: I love you my Lord.

(the both passionately embraced each other, the bride burst in tears not knowing why exactly but she could feel the emotions of her groom. At this time the fate of this love has been decided, the groom must lay off his life if he wishes his beloved to live else she has to die as payment for the debt she owes.)

Solace

The bride has nowhere to turn as her sorrow greatly increased she has no idea what's about to happen but fears her love might not last, her tears roll like the water fall of a ventilated garden, her wail was like the mourning of a thousand women, on hearing this her friend came around to console her, yet her words could not heal the brokenness of a broken heart.

Friend: I came as soon as I heard your call, I beseech you, tell me what is this that troubles you.

Bride: the dances of the trees have stopped for the songs of be wind is quiet, birds are silent and cold even in the hot summer sun

Friend: speak to me mi lady, your words I hear but understanding I do not have

Bride: the sun shines yet my world is dark, how can I be so dry and thirsty when a downpour of rain is on me.

Friend: I have heard this song before and it was when your parents left, tell me, who is leaving?

Bride: I'm afraid my beloved is leaving me, of what use is my life, perhaps death is all I deserve.

Friend: say no such thing, if there is anything I'm certain of is that he loves you and will not want to leave.

Bride: he doesn't want to leave but I'm afraid something is making him to.

Friend: take heart my friend, I am sure all of this has a reason.

Bride: what shall I do, how shall my life be, to whom shall I go? I can no longer leave like this I can't

Friend: (embraces her) everything will be fine calm down.

Comfort

The groom employs the hands of the light to watch over his bride

Groom: you've done well; much recommendation I have heard about you but one more thing I beseech you do for me.

Light: anything my lord and I shall be unto it.

Groom: the all father has granted that in the eventuality of a lover's sacrifice, the love they share shall leave beyond time if they party for whom they died live life worthy the two shall be reunited again.

Light: thanks to the all father, this is a relieve news to a troubled soul.

Groom: indeed.

Light: away I must go your bride I shall call for this news shall gladden her heart

Groom: no light I beseech you, speak not of this until the passing is done, in a few hours my execution shall begin and then shall she be informed lest her heart fails.

Light: but my lord

Groom: this favor I ask, that you keep my bride pure until we are reunited in the next life.

Light: my lord I shall be about this as you request but I insist that your beloved be informed.

Groom: very well then, you may inform her but not before my execution.

Light: very well my lord I must check on her then to know how she fares.

Groom: on your way, be gone may the all father be with you.

Ice Bridge

Wallowing in her demise, lost and confuse the bride has no idea what to do, she eventually thought to herself she cannot keep leaving like this unloved by all and the one who truly loved her is about to be taken so she decided to end her life by hanging when suddenly Light appeared

Light: the all father forbids you, (he holds her and pull the rope off her) what are you doing?

Bride: (with a sober sound of tear she responded) allow me oh light for nothing I am worthy of, my death shall do good to the inhabitants of the earth.

Light: far be it from you to think this, this your worth you do not know has set a man to die for you.

Bride: my beloved, what are you saying

Light: I am forbidden from speaking of this before it is time

Bride: may the all father strike you dead if your mouth remains shut, I beseech you oh light. lighten my burden.

Light: mi lady sit and hear of me for the matters here are weightier than I

Bride: sited I am please indulge me.

Light: many, many years ago before the passing of your parent… you..

Bride: my parent did not pass they left me, they abandoned me

Light: that's what is seemed and so you were told so your life can be spared.

Bride: what are saying?

Light: before your parent died, your lineage was in a debt that could not be payed, therefore the debtor made a deal with your ancestors that every child that come of age in your family shall pay a stipulated amount to offset the debt, but your parent were unable to as their parent and their grandparent and the consequences shall be death if the payment is not made. This is why your parent left you so that the debtor may not know about you but in their race the debtor caught up with them and they did die.

Bride: if what you say is true then what's my case in this.

Light: the deal with the debtor only ends when the last of the bloodline is dead and that last…

Bride: I am… (looking surprised and amazed she knew not what to do). Then what has my beloved to do with this?

Light: this case was before the all father and your beloved, my lord was there, the pain of having to watch you die was tearing him apart he could not bear to leave without you so he made a deal in your place and traded his life for yours in that way your debt is paid.

Bride: oh just love… it should be me, no, no, no I cannot let this where is he I must see him.

Light: hear me mi lady in the case of this sacrifice the all father decreed that the two lovers shall be reunited again should the one for whom he died live a life that is worthy.

Bride: oh light I beseech you take me to my beloved (with rivers of tears flowing down her eye she kept pleading)

(light eventually took her as the both walked away to the execution grounds)

Beyound Words

Light and the bride walked a long distance running and weeping wishing it was not true, she stumbled and fell yet nothing could stand in her way, the desire to see her beloved well in her an ocean of thirst that cannot be quenched but on reaching the execution arena her beloved had already been executed.

Bride: (weeping and crying uncontrollably) my lord what is this you have done? It should have been me

Groom: (with a strong gasp for breath he replied) you wish to leave me alone in this vast world.

Bride: is that not same you've done to me?

Groom: no my love, for this I have done we shall meet again we shall be reunited our heart shall echo our names in eternity.

Bride: why, why, why have you done this how sure are you that I love you and deserve your life in death?

Groom: I do not offer myself because you love me, I did because I love you. What is love when it loves not the unloved? Listen my love, I have loved you with an everlasting love and not even death shall put an end to it.

Bride: oh my lord (weeping profusely)

Groom: weep no more for your death I die that my life you may live and here after we shall be together again

I have loved you with an everlasting love.

(with this words the groom lowered his head as his spirit passes away from his body the bride could not hold her grief but yet vow to live a life worthy so in the end she could be with her beloved.)

The Conclusion

And so it was that considering not our opinion Jesus took upon himself to pay off the debt our lives owe so we could be free and in this freedom we could live his life as he died our death.

Just as the all father have said all of those who lived worthily after the sacrifice of the groom shall be considered the lamb's Bride and in the realm beyond time they shall be reunited and their love shall bloom like the flowers of the garden.

Do you live worthy of his love? Do you think you can see him or be with him? Do you think you will be reunited with him?

Remember he loves you just the way you are, all you need to do is accept him, believe in his work on the cross and his life shall you have and then shall you be reunited with him in the world to come else the debtor shall come and for the debt you cannot pay, your life will be required and in eternal condemnation shall you spend eternity.

Giving a thought on all of this, make this decision today as you accept his sacrifice for you so you could get his life.

"lord Jesus, come into my life, I receive you today, be my lord and savior, I believe you died for me, grant me your life, I reject the way of sin and Satan I receive the way of life. This day I am a born again this day I return to you, receive me lord Jesus. Amen"

Congratulations, if you just prayed that prayer God bless, find a bible believing and holy spirit filled church to attend.

Send us a message via these route:

emmanuelinalegwu@gmail.com

About the Author

Inalegwu Adakole Emmanuel

Inalegwu Adakole Emmanuel is a prolific writer and speaker, he has spoken in conventions, crusades, conferences and other gatherings. Among other expertise he writes.